THE ADVENTURES OF OLD MAN COYOTE

THE ADVENTURES OF OLD MAN COYOTE

THORNTON W. BURGESS

Cover Illustration by Tricia Zimic

AERIE

CONTENTS

CONTENTS

I

THE STRANGE VOICE

Listen!" It was Jimmy Skunk speaking. He had just met Peter Rabbit halfway down the Crooked Little Path just where the moonlight was brightest. But he did not need to tell Peter to listen. Peter *was* listening— listening with all his might. He was sitting up very straight, and his long ears were turned in the direction of the strange sound. Just then it came again, a sound such as neither Peter Rabbit nor Jimmy Skunk had ever heard before. Peter's teeth began to chatter.

"Wha—wha—what is it?" he whispered.

"I don't know, unless it is Hooty the Owl gone crazy," replied Jimmy.

"No," said Peter, "it isn't Hooty the Owl. Hooty never could make such a noise as that."

"Maybe it's Dippy the Loon. I've heard him on the Big River, and he sounds just as if he had gone crazy," replied Jimmy.

"No," said Peter, looking behind him nervously. "No, it isn't Dippy the Loon, for Dippy never leaves the water, and that voice came from the Green Meadows. I wouldn't be surprised—" Peter didn't finish, for just then the strange voice sounded again, and it was nearer than before. Never had the Green Meadows or the Green Forest heard anything like it. It sounded something like Hooty the Owl, and Dippy the Loon, and two or three little dogs howling all together, and there was something in the sound that made cold chills run up and down

Peter Rabbit's backbone. He crept a little closer to Jimmy Skunk.

"I believe it is Farmer Brown's boy and some of his friends laughing and shouting together," said Jimmy.

"No, it isn't! Farmer Brown's boy and his friends can make some dreadful noises but nothing so dreadful as that. It makes me afraid, Jimmy Skunk," said Peter.

"Pooh! You're afraid of your own shadow!" replied Jimmy Skunk, who isn't afraid of much of anything. "Let's go down there and find out what it is."

Peter's big eyes grew rounder than ever with fright at the very thought. "D-d-don't you think of such a thing, Jimmy Skunk! D-d-don't y-y-you think of such a thing!" he chattered. "I know it's something terrible. Oh, dear! I wish I were safe at home in the dear Old Briarpatch."

Again sounded the strange voice, or was it voices? It seemed sometimes as if there were two or three together. Then again it sounded like only one. Each time Peter Rabbit crept a little closer to Jimmy Skunk. Pretty soon even Jimmy began to feel a little uneasy.

"I'm going home," said he suddenly.

"I want to, but I don't dare to," said Peter, shaking all over with fright.

"Pooh! Anyone who can run as fast as you can ought not to be afraid," said Jimmy. "But if you really are afraid, you can come up to my house and stay a while," he added, good-naturedly.

"Oh, thank you, Jimmy Skunk. I believe I will come sit on your doorstep if you don't mind."

So together they went up to Jimmy Skunk's house, and sat on his doorstep in the moonlight, and listened to the

strange voice all the long night; and then, when he saw Old Mother West Wind coming down from the Purple Hills in the early dawn, Peter Rabbit became courageous enough to start for his home in the dear Old Briar-patch.

II

∽∽∽

Peter Rabbit's Run for Life

It was very, very early in the morning when Old Mother West Wind came down from the Purple Hills with her big bag and out of it emptied her children, the Merry Little Breezes, to play on the Green Meadows. Peter Rabbit, watching her from the doorstep of Jimmy Skunk's house, felt his courage grow. All the night long he and Jimmy Skunk had sat on the doorstep listening to a strange voice, a terrible voice Peter had thought. But with the first light of the coming day the voice had been heard no more, and now, as Peter watched Old Mother West Wind just as he had done so often before, he began to wonder if

that dreadful voice hadn't been a bad dream.

So he bade Jimmy Skunk good-by, and started for his home in the dear Old Briar-patch. He wanted to run just as fast as he knew how, but he didn't. No, Sir, he didn't. That is, not while he was in sight of Jimmy Skunk. You see, he knew that Jimmy would laugh at him. He wasn't brave enough to be laughed at.

> The bravest boy is not the one
>   Who does some mighty deed;
> Who risks his very life perchance
>   To serve another's need.
> The bravest boy is he who dares
>   To face the scornful laugh
> For doing what he knows is right,
>   Though others mock and chaff.

But as soon as Peter was sure that Jimmy Skunk could no longer see him,

he began to hurry, and the nearer he got to the Old Briar-patch, the faster he hurried. He would run a little way as fast as he could, lipperty-lipperty-lip, and then stop and look and listen nervously. Then he would do it all over again. It was one of these times when he was listening that Peter thought he heard a soft footstep behind him. It sounded very much like the footstep of Reddy Fox. Peter crouched down very low and sat perfectly still, holding his breath and straining his ears. There it was again, pit-a-pat, pit-a-pat, very soft and coming nearer. Peter waited no longer. He sprang forward with a great leap and started for the dear Old Briar-patch as fast as he could go, which, you know, is very fast indeed. As he ran, he saw behind him a fierce, grinning face. It was very much like the face of Reddy Fox,

only larger and fiercer and gray instead of red.

Never in all his life had Peter run as he did now, for he knew that he was running for his life. It seemed as if those long legs of his hardly touched the ground. He didn't dare try any of the tricks with which he had so often fooled Reddy Fox, for he didn't know anything about this terrible stranger. He might not be fooled by tricks as Reddy Fox was.

Peter began to breathe hard. It seemed to him that he could feel the hot breath of the fierce stranger. And right down inside, Peter somehow felt sure that this was the owner of the strange voice which had so frightened him in the night. Snap! That was a pair of cruel jaws right at his very heels. It gave Peter new strength, and he made longer jumps than before. The dear Old Briar-patch, the safe Old Briar-patch, was just

ahead. With three mighty jumps, Peter reached the opening of one of his own private little paths and dived in under a bramble bush. And even as he did so, he heard the clash of sharp teeth and felt some hair pulled from his tail. And then, outside the Old Briar-patch, broke forth that same terrible voice Peter had heard in the night.

Peter didn't stop to look at the stranger, but hurried to the very middle of the Old Briar-patch and there he stretched out at full length and panted and panted for breath.

III

REDDY FOX MAKES A DISCOVERY

Reddy Fox had boasted that he was not afraid of the unknown stranger who had frightened Peter Rabbit so, and whose voice in the night had brought the great fear to the Green Meadows and the Green Forest. But Reddy Fox is always boasting, and a boaster is seldom very brave. Right down deep in his heart Reddy *was* afraid. What he was afraid of, he didn't know. That is one reason that he was afraid. He is always afraid of things that he doesn't know about. Old Granny Fox had taught Reddy that.

"If you are afraid of things you don't know all about, and just keep away from

them, they never will hurt you," said wise old Granny Fox, and that is one reason that Farmer Brown's boy had never been able to catch her in a trap. But Granny was too smart to boast that she wasn't afraid when she was, while Reddy was forever bragging of how brave he was, when all the time he was one of the greatest cowards among all the little meadow and forest people.

When he had first heard that strange voice, little cold chills had chased each other up and down his backbone, just as they had with nearly all the others who had heard it, and Reddy had not gone hunting that night. But Reddy has a big appetite, and a hungry stomach doesn't let one think of much else. So after a day or two, Reddy, grew brave enough to go hunting. Somehow he had a feeling that it was safer to hunt during the day instead of during the night. You see, it was

only after jolly, round, red Mr. Sun had
gone to bed behind the Purple Hills that
that strange voice was heard, and Reddy
guessed that perhaps the stranger slept
during the day.

So Reddy started out very early in the
morning, stepping as softly as he knew
how, looking behind every bush and tree,
and with his sharp little ears wide open
to catch every sound. Every few feet he
stopped and sniffed the wind very carefully, for Reddy's nose can tell him of
things which his eyes do not see and his
ears do not hear. And all the time he was
ready to run at the first sign of danger.
He had left the Green Forest and was
out on the Green Meadows, hoping to
catch Danny Meadow Mouse, when that
sharp little nose of his was tickled by
one of the Merry Little Breezes with a
smell that Reddy knew. Reddy turned
and went in the direction from which the

13

Merry Little Breeze had come. Just a few steps he went, and then he stopped and sniffed.

"Um-m-m," said Reddy to himself, "that smells to me like chicken. It certainly does smell like chicken!"

Very, very slowly and carefully Reddy moved forward in the direction from which that delicious smell came. Every few steps he stopped and sniffed. Sniff, sniff, sniff! Yes, it certainly was chicken. Reddy's mouth watered. A few more steps and there, a little way in front of him, partly hidden in a clump of tall grass and bushes, lay a half-eaten chicken. Reddy stopped short and sat down to look at it. Then he looked all around it to see if there was anyone about. Then he walked clear around it in a circle, but he was very careful not to go too near. Finally he sat down again where he could smell the chicken. His

tongue hung out with longing, and water dripped from the corners of his mouth. His stomach said, "Go get it"; but his head said, "Don't go any nearer; it may be some sort of a trap."

Then Reddy remembered one of the sayings of wise old Granny Fox:

"When you are tempted very much
Just turn your back and go away.
Temptation then can harm you not,
But only those who choose to stay."

"I hate to do it, but I guess it's the best way," said Reddy Fox and turned his back on the chicken and trotted away.

15

IV

REDDY FOX CONSULTS BOBBY COON

When Reddy Fox had turned his back on the half-eaten chicken that he had found hidden in a bunch of grass and bushes on the Green Meadows it had been the hardest thing to do that Reddy could remember, for his stomach fairly ached, he was so hungry. But there might be danger there, and it was best to be safe. So Reddy turned and trotted away where he could neither see nor smell that chicken. He caught some grasshoppers, and he found a family of fat beetles. They were not very filling, but they were better than nothing. After a while he felt better, and he curled up in a warm sunny spot to rest and think.

"It may be that Farmer Brown's boy has set a trap there," said Reddy to himself. Then he remembered that the chicken was half-eaten, and he knew that it wasn't likely that Farmer Brown's boy would have a half-eaten chicken unless he had found one that Jimmy Skunk had left near the hen-yard, and for some reason he didn't know, he had a feeling that Jimmy Skunk had not had anything to do with that chicken. The more he thought about it, the more he felt sure that that chicken had something to do with the stranger whose voice had brought so much fear to the Green Meadows. The very thought made him nervous and spoiled his sun-bath.

"I believe I'll run over and see Bobby Coon," said Reddy, and off he started for the Green Forest.

Bobby Coon had been out all night,

but he had not been very far away from his hollow-tree, because he too had felt little chills of fear when he heard that strange voice, which wasn't the voice of Hooty the Owl or of Dippy the Loon or of a little yelping dog and yet sounded something like all three together. So Bobby's stomach wasn't as full as usual, and he felt cross and uncomfortable. You know it is hard work to feel hungry and pleasant at the same time. He had just begun to doze when he heard Reddy Fox calling softly at the foot of the tree.

"Bobby! Bobby Coon!" called Reddy.

Bobby didn't answer. He kept perfectly still to try to make Reddy think that he was asleep. But Reddy kept right on calling. Finally Bobby scrambled up to the doorway of his house in the big hollow-tree and scowled down at Reddy Fox.

"Well, what is it?" he snapped crossly.

"You ought to be ashamed of yourself to disturb people who are trying to get a little honest sleep."

Reddy grinned. "I'm very sorry to wake you up, Bobby Coon," said Reddy, "but you see I want your advice. I know that there is no one smarter than you, and I have just discovered something very important about which I want to know what you think."

The scowl disappeared from Bobby Coon's face. He felt very much flattered, just as Reddy meant that he should feel, and he tried to look very important and wise as he said:

"I'm listening, Reddy Fox. What is it that is so important?"

Then Reddy told him all about the half-eaten chicken over on the Green Meadows, and how he suspected that the stranger with the terrible voice had had

19

something to do with it. Bobby listened gravely.

"Pooh!" said he. "Probably Jimmy Skunk knows something about it."

"No," replied Reddy, "I'm sure that Jimmy Skunk doesn't know anything about it. Come over with me and see it for yourself."

Bobby began to back down into his house. "You'll have to excuse me this morning, Reddy Fox. You see, I'm very tired and need sleep," said he.

Reddy turned his head aside to hide a smile, for he knew that Bobby was afraid.

"I'm sure it must have been Jimmy Skunk," continued Bobby. "Why don't you go ask him? I never like to meddle with other people's business."

And with that Bobby Coon backed down out of sight in the hollow-tree.

V

Reddy Fox Visits Jimmy Skunk

Bobby Coon is afraid! Yes, Sir, Bobby Coon is afraid! He doesn't dare go with me to look at that half-eaten chicken over on the Green Meadows. He's a coward, that's what he is!"

Reddy Fox muttered this to himself as he trotted away from Bobby Coon's big hollow-tree in the Green Forest. Reddy was right, and he was wrong. He was right in thinking that Bobby Coon was afraid. Bobby *was* afraid, but that didn't make him a coward. You see, he couldn't see what good it would do him to go see that half-eaten chicken way out there in the Green Meadows so far away from

trees. Bobby is like Happy Jack Squirrel—he never feels really safe unless
there is a tree close at hand to climb, for
Bobby's legs are not very long, and
though he can run fast for a little distance, he soon gets out of breath. Then
he climbs the nearest tree. But if there
had been any really good reason for going, Bobby would have gone even though
he was afraid, and that shows that he
wasn't a coward.

But Reddy Fox likes to think himself
very brave and everyone else a coward.
So he trotted along with his nose turned
up in scorn because Bobby Coon was
afraid. He was disappointed, too, was
Reddy Fox. You see he had hoped to get
Bobby to go with him and when they got
there that Bobby would go close to the
half-eaten chicken and try to find out
who had left it on the Green Meadows,
and for what reason. Reddy, who is al-

22

ways suspicious, thought that there might be a trap, and if so, Bobby would find it, and then Reddy would know without running any danger himself. That shows how sly he is.

But as long as Bobby wouldn't go, there was nothing for Reddy to do but to try the same plan with Jimmy Skunk, and so he headed straight for Jimmy Skunk's house. Now deep down in his heart Reddy Fox hated Jimmy Skunk, and more than once he had tried to get Jimmy into trouble. But now, as he saw Jimmy sitting on his doorstep, Reddy looked as pleasant as only Reddy can. He smiled as if Jimmy were his very best friend.

"Good morning, Jimmy Skunk. I'm glad to see you," said Reddy. "I hope you are feeling well this morning."

Now Jimmy had had a good breakfast of fat beetles, and he was feeling very

good-natured. But he wasn't fooled by Reddy's pleasant ways. To himself he thought, "I wonder what mischief Reddy Fox is up to," but aloud he said:

"Good morning, Reddy Fox. You are looking very fine and handsome this morning. Of course no one who is as big and brave as you are is afraid of the stranger with the terrible voice who has frightened the rest of us so for the last few nights."

Now all the time he was saying this, Jimmy knew perfectly well that Reddy was afraid, and he turned his head to hide a smile as Reddy swelled up to look very big and important and replied:

"Oh, my, no! No, indeed, certainly not! I'm not afraid of anybody or anything. By the way, I saw a strange thing down on the Green Meadows early this morning. It was a half-eaten chicken hidden

in a clump of grass and bushes. I wondered if you left it there."

Jimmy Skunk pricked up his ears. "No," said he, "I didn't leave it there. I haven't taken a chicken from Farmer Brown's this spring, and I haven't been up to his hen-house for more than a week. Who do you suppose could have left it there?"

"I haven't the least idea unless—" Reddy looked this way and that to make sure that they were alone—"unless it was the stranger who has frightened everyone but me," he finished in a whisper.

Jimmy pricked his ears up more than ever. "Do you really suppose it could have been?" he asked.

"Come down there with me and see for yourself," replied Reddy. And Jimmy said he would.

VI

JIMMY SKUNK GOES WITH REDDY FOX

Jimmy Skunk and Reddy Fox trotted along down the Crooked Little Path to the Green Meadows. Reddy was impatient and in a hurry. But Jimmy Skunk never hurries, and he didn't now. He just took his time, and Reddy Fox had to keep waiting for him. Reddy was nervous and anxious. He kept turning his head this way and that way. He looked behind every little bush and clump of grass. He cocked his sharp ears at every little sound. He sniffed every little breeze. It was very plain that Reddy Fox was ill at ease.

"Hurry up, Jimmy Skunk! Hurry up!" he urged every few minutes, and he had

hard work to make his voice sound pleasant.

But Jimmy didn't hurry. Indeed, it seemed as if Jimmy were slower than usual. The more impatient Reddy grew, the slower Jimmy seemed to go. And every time Reddy's back was turned, Jimmy would grin, and his sharp little eyes twinkled with mischief. You see, he knew that despite all his boasting Reddy Fox *was* afraid, and because he wasn't afraid himself, Jimmy was getting a lot of fun out of watching Reddy. Once, when Reddy had stopped to look over the Green Meadows, Jimmy stole up behind him very softly and suddenly pulled Reddy's tail. Reddy sprang forward with a frightened yelp and started to run as only Reddy can. Then he heard Jimmy Skunk laughing and knew that Jimmy had played a joke on him. He stopped short and whirled around.

27

"What are you laughing at, Jimmy Skunk?" he shouted angrily.

"Oh, nothing, nothing at all," replied Jimmy, and his face was as sober as if he never had laughed and never could laugh. Reddy opened his mouth to say something ugly, but suddenly remembered that if he quarrelled with Jimmy Skunk, then Jimmy wouldn't go any farther with him. So he gulped down his anger as best he could and grinned sheepishly while he waited for Jimmy to catch up with him.

So at last they came to the bunch of grass and bushes in which Reddy had found the half-eaten chicken early that morning. There it lay just as Reddy had left it. Reddy stopped at a safe distance and pointed it out to Jimmy Skunk. Jimmy looked at it thoughtfully.

"Who do you suppose could have brought it away down here on the Green

Meadows?" whispered Reddy, as if afraid that someone might overhear him.

Jimmy Skunk scratched his head as if thinking very hard. "It might have been Redtail the Hawk," said he at last.

"That's so. I didn't think of him," replied Reddy.

"But it looks to me as if it were left there in the night, and Redtail never hunts at night because his eyes are for seeing in the daytime and not in the dark," added Jimmy Skunk. "Let's go closer, and perhaps we can tell who left it there."

"Of course. That's a good idea," replied Reddy, starting forward as if he were going to walk right up to the chicken. After a few steps he stopped as if he had a sudden thought. "I tell you what," said he "one of us had better keep watch to see that no danger is near. I am taller than you and can see over the grass bet-

ter than you can, so I'll keep watch while you see what you can find out."

Now Jimmy Skunk saw through Reddy's plan right away, but Jimmy wasn't afraid, because he isn't afraid of much of anything, so he agreed. While Reddy kept watch, he carefully made his way to the half-eaten chicken hidden in the clump of grass and bushes. All the time he kept his eyes wide open for traps. But there were no traps there. He was gone a long time, and when at last he came out, his face was very sober.

"Well, was it Redtail the Hawk?" asked Reddy eagerly.

"No," said Jimmy. "No, it wasn't Redtail the Hawk or Hooty the Owl. It was someone with teeth very much like yours, Reddy Fox, only bigger, and with feet very much like yours, only these were bigger too. And the chicken wasn't one of Farmer Brown's at all; it was

brought from somewhere farther away than Farmer Brown's, and that shows that it was someone smarter than you, Reddy Fox, because whoever it was knew that if they stole a chicken from Farmer Brown, his boy and Bowser the Hound, would come looking for it."

VII

A CALL ON DIGGER THE BADGER

For fox or man the better plan
    With unknown danger near,
Is to go home and no more roam
    Until the way be clear.

That is what Reddy Fox thinks. The thought popped right into his head when Jimmy Skunk told him that the half-eaten chicken had been left on the Green Meadows by some one with teeth and feet very like Reddy's own but bigger. But Reddy pretended not to believe it. "Pooh!" said he. "How do you know that this stranger has feet like mine, only bigger. You haven't seen him, have you?"

"No," said Jimmy Skunk, shaking his head, "no, I haven't seen him, and I don't need to, to know that. His footprints are right over here in the sand. Come look for yourself, Reddy Fox."

"No, thanks!" said Reddy hastily. "The fact is, I have some very important matters to look after in the Green Forest, and I must hurry along. You'll excuse me, won't you, Jimmy Skunk? If you say that there are footprints like mine, only larger, of course I believe it. I would stop to look at them if I could, but I find that I am already very late. By the way, if you will look a little closer at those footprints, I think you will find that they were made by a dog. I'm sorry I can't wait for you, but you are such a slow walker that I really haven't the time. Let me know if you find out anything about this stranger." And with that off he started for the Green Forest.

Jimmy Skunk grinned, for he knew that Reddy had nothing more important to attend to than to get away as fast as he could from a place which he felt might be dangerous.

"Don't fool yourself, Reddy Fox, by thinking I don't know the footprints of a dog when I see them. Besides, I smelled of them, and they don't smell of dog!" shouted Jimmy, before Reddy could get out of hearing.

Jimmy watched Reddy out of sight and chuckled as he saw Reddy keep turning to look over his shoulder as if he expected to find something terrible at his heels. "I'd never run away until I knew what I was running from!" exclaimed Jimmy, with the greatest scorn. "Did you ever see such a coward?"

With Reddy gone, Jimmy's thoughts came back to the queer things which were driving all the happiness from the

Green Meadows at the very happiest time of all the year. There was that strange, terrible voice in the night, the voice that was not that of Hooty the Owl or Dippy the Loon or a little yelping dog, yet which sounded something like all three, and which was frightening all the little people until they were afraid to move out of sight of their homes. And here was this half-eaten chicken hidden in the clump of grass and bushes on the Green Meadows by someone with teeth and feet very much like those of Reddy Fox only bigger. It was all very queer, very queer indeed. The more he thought about it, the more Jimmy felt sure that the owner of the terrible voice was the owner of the big teeth and the maker of the strange footprints. He was scratching his head as he puzzled over the matter when he happened to look over to the

home of Digger the Badger. Jimmy's eyes brightened.

"I believe I'll make a call on Digger. Perhaps he will know something about it," said he, and off he started.

Digger the Badger sat on his doorstep. He has very few friends, for he is grumpy and very apt to be out of sorts. Besides, most of the little meadow people are afraid of him. But Jimmy Skunk isn't afraid of anyone but Farmer Brown's boy, and not even of him unless he has his terrible gun. So he walked right up to the doorstep where Digger the Badger was sitting.

"Good morning," said Jimmy politely.

"Morning," grunted Digger the Badger.

"What do you think of the queer doings on the Green Meadows?" asked Jimmy.

"What queer doings?" asked Digger.

Then Jimmy Skunk told all about the strange voice and the strange footprints.

Digger the Badger didn't say a word until Jimmy was through. Then he chuckled.

"Why," said he, "that is only my old friend from the Great West—Old Man Coyote."

VIII

OLD MAN COYOTE MAKES HIMSELF AT HOME

It was out at last. Digger the Badger had told Jimmy Skunk who it was that had so frightened the little people of the Green Forest and the Green Meadows with his terrible voice, and Jimmy Skunk had straightway sent the Merry Little Breezes of Old Mother West Wind over to the Smiling Pool, up along the Laughing Brook, through the Green Forest, and over the Green Meadows to spread the news that it was Old Man Coyote from the Great West who had come to make his home on the Green Meadows. And that night when they heard his voice, somehow it didn't sound so terrible. You see, they knew who it

was, and that made all the difference in
the world.

> The shivers still might crawl and creep
>   And chase away good friendly Sleep,
> But knowing whom he had to fear
>   Brought to each heart a bit of cheer.

That may seem a bit queer, but it was
so. You see, not knowing what or whom
to be afraid of made the little meadow
and forest people afraid every minute of
the time, afraid to sleep, afraid to put
their noses out of their homes, almost
afraid to draw a long breath. But now
that they knew it was Old Man Coyote
who had so frightened them, they felt
better, for Digger the Badger, who had
known him in the Great West where
they had been neighbors, had told
Jimmy Skunk what he looked like, and
Jimmy Skunk had spread the news so

that everybody would know Old Man Coyote when they saw him. So though each one knew that he mustn't give Old Man Coyote a chance to catch him, each felt sure right down in his heart that all he had to do was to be just a little bit smarter than Old Man Coyote, and he would be safe.

Of course it didn't take Old Man Coyote long to learn that he had been found out. He grinned to himself, stretched, and yawned, and then came out from his secret hiding place.

"I think I'll call on my neighbors," said he, and trotted towards the house of Digger the Badger. The Merry Little Breezes saw him first and in a great flutter of excitement they hurried this way and that way to tell everybody that the stranger from the Great West had come out in the light of day. My, my, my! such a scampering as there was for a

safe place from which to peep out at Old Man Coyote! He pretended not to notice, and didn't look this way or that way, but trotted on about his own business.

Digger the Badger was sitting on his doorstep, and he grinned when he saw Old Man Coyote coming.

"It's about time you called on your old friend," said he.

It was Old Man Coyote's turn to grin. "That's so, Brother Badger," he replied, "but the fact is, I've been living very quietly."

"Excepting at night," said Digger, showing all his teeth in a rather broad grin. "You're voice certainly has sounded good to me."

"I guess it's the first time," interrupted Old Man Coyote.

"The first time I heard it I thought I was dreaming," continued Digger, just as if he hadn't heard what Old Man Coyote

41

said. "Seems just like home to have you about. But tell me, how does it happen that you have come here out of the Great West?"

"That's too long a story to tell now. Anyway, I might ask you the same thing. But here I am, and I believe I'll stay. I like the Green Meadows and the Green Forest. Now I must be going along to call on the rest of my new neighbors. I hope they'll be glad to see me." Old Man Coyote grinned again when he said this, for no one knew better than he did how very much afraid of him his new neighbors were.

"Come again when you can stop longer," said Digger the Badger.

"I will," replied Old Man Coyote, starting toward the Smiling Pool.

IX

OLD MAN COYOTE MEETS REDDY FOX

No matter how you feel inside
  Hold up your head! Call up your pride!
Stand fast! Look brave! Then none will guess
  The fear you feel, but won't confess.

Jimmy Skunk learned this when he was a very little fellow. Now he isn't afraid of much of anything, but there was a time when he was. Oh, my, yes! There was a time when he first started out to see the world, and before he had found out that all the world is afraid of that little bag of scent he always carries with him, when Jimmy often was as frightened as Peter Rabbit ever is, and you know Peter is very eas-

ily frightened. But Jimmy used to think of that little verse, and though sometimes he had to shut his mouth as tightly as he knew how to keep his teeth from chattering with fear, he would hold up his head, stand fast, and look brave. What do you think happened? Why, in a little while people began to say that Jimmy Skunk wasn't afraid of anything, and so no one tried to bother him. Of course when he found this out, Jimmy wasn't afraid.

But Reddy Fox is different. He dearly loves to tell how brave he is. He brags and boasts. But when he finds himself in a place where he is afraid, he shows it. Yes, Sir, he shows it. Reddy Fox has never learned to stand fast and look brave. When Reddy had first been told that the stranger with the voice which had sounded so terrible in the night was Old Man Coyote from the Great West,

and that he had decided to make his home on the Green Meadows, Reddy had said: "Pooh! I'm not afraid of him!" and had swelled himself up and strutted back and forth as if he really meant it. But all the time Reddy took care, the very greatest care, to keep out of the way of Old Man Coyote.

Of course, someone told Digger the Badger what Reddy had said, and Digger told Old Man Coyote, who just grinned and said nothing. But he noticed how careful Reddy was to keep out of his way, and he made up his mind that he would like to meet Reddy and find out how brave he really was. So one moonlight night he hid behind a big log near one of Reddy's favorite hunting places. Pretty soon Reddy came tiptoeing along, watching for foolish young mice. Just a little while before he had heard the voice of Old Man Coyote way over on the edge

of the Old Pasture, so he never once thought of meeting him here. Just as he passed the end of the old log, a deep voice in the black shadow said:

"Good evening, Brother Fox."

Reddy whirled about. His heart seemed to come right up in his throat. It was too late to run, for there was Old Man Coyote right in front of him. Reddy tried to swell himself up just as he so often did before the little people who were afraid of him, but somehow he couldn't. "Go-good evening, Mr Coyote," he replied, but his voice sounded very weak. "I hear you've come to make your home on the Green Meadows. I-I hope we will be the best of friends."

"Of course we will," replied Old Man Coyote. "I'm always the best of friends with those who are not afraid of me, and I hear that you are not afraid of anybody."

"N-no, I-I'm not afraid of anybody," said Reddy. "Everybody is afraid of me." All the time he was speaking, he was slowly backing away, and in spite of his bold words, he was shaking with fear. Old Man Coyote saw it and he chuckled to himself.

"I'm not, Brother Fox!" he suddenly snapped, in a deep, horrid sounding voice. "Gr-r-r-r-r, I'm not!" As he said it, all the hair along his back stood on end, and he showed all his great, cruel-looking teeth.

Instead of holding his ground as Jimmy Skunk would have done, Reddy leaped backward, tripped over his own tail, fell, and then scrambled to his feet with a frightened yelp, and ran as he had never run before in all his life. And as he ran, he heard Old Man Coyote laughing, and all the Green Meadows

and the Green Forest heard it:

"Ho, ho, ho! Ha, ha, ha! Hee, hee, hee! Ho, ha, hee, ho! Reddy Fox isn't afraid! Ho, ho!"

Reddy ground his teeth in rage, but he kept on running.

X

GRANNY FOX VISITS PRICKLY PORKY

"I've often heard old Granny say:
  'He longest lives who runs away.'"

Reddy Fox didn't realize that he
was speaking aloud. He was trying to make himself think that he
wasn't a coward and that in running
away from Old Man Coyote he had done
only what every one of the little meadow
and forest people would have done in his
place. So, without knowing it, he had
spoken aloud.

"But he who runs must leave behind
  His self-respect and peace of mind."

The voice came from right over Reddy's head, but he didn't have to look up to know who was there. It was Sammy Jay, of course. Sammy is always on hand when he isn't wanted, and Reddy knew by the look in his eyes that Sammy knew about the meeting with Old Man Coyote.

"What are you waiting around here for?" asked Reddy, with a snarl.

"To tell Old Granny Fox how brave you are," retorted Sammy Jay, his eyes sparkling with mischief, "and how fast you can run."

"You'd better mind your own affairs and leave mine alone. I shall tell Granny all about it myself, anyway," snapped Reddy.

Now when Reddy said that, he didn't tell the truth, for he had no intention of telling Old Granny Fox of how he had run from Old Man Coyote, but hardly

were the words out of his mouth when
old Granny Fox herself stepped out from
behind a bush. She had been up in the
Old Pasture for a week or two and had
just come back, so she knew nothing of
the fright which Old Man Coyote had
given those who live in the Green Meadows and the Green Forest.

"I'm all ready to listen right now,
Reddy," said she.

Reddy hung his head. He coughed and
cleared his throat and tried to think of
some way out of it. But it was of no use.
There sat Sammy Jay ready to tell if he
didn't, and so, mumbling so low that
twice Granny told him to speak louder,
Reddy told how he had run, and how Old
Man Coyote had laughed at him so that
all the little people in the Green Forest
and on the Green Meadows had heard.

"Of course he laughed!" snapped old
Granny Fox. "You're a coward, Reddy

Fox, just a plain coward. It's all well enough to run away when you know you have to, but to run before there is anything to be afraid of shows you are the biggest kind of a coward. Bah! Get out of my sight!"

Reddy slunk away, muttering to himself and glaring angrily at Sammy Jay, who was chuckling with delight to see Reddy looking so uncomfortable. Old Granny Fox made sure that Reddy was out of sight, and then she sat down to think, and there was a worried pucker in her forehead.

"Old Man Coyote is a wolf," said she, talking to herself, "and a wolf on the Green Meadows and in the Green Forest will mean hard hunting for Reddy and me when food is scarce. It is of no use for me to fight him, for he is bigger and stronger than I am. I'll just have to make all the trouble for him that I can,

and then perhaps he'll go away. I wonder if he has ever met Prickly Porky the Porcupine. I believe I'll go over and make Prickly Porky a call right now!"

And as she trotted through the Green Forest on her way to call on Prickly Porky, her thoughts were very busy, very busy indeed. She was planning trouble for Old Man Coyote.

XI

<hr>

GRANNY FOX TELLS PRICKLY PORKY A STORY

A little tale which isn't true,
  And eager ears to heed it,
Means trouble starts right there to brew
  With tattle-tales to feed it.

No one knows how true this is better than does old Granny Fox. And no one knows better than she how to make trouble for other people by starting little untrue stories. You see, she learned long ago how fast a mean little tale will travel once it has been started, and so when there is someone with whom she is afraid to fight honestly, she uses these little untrue tales instead of claws and teeth, and often

they hurt a great deal worse than claws or teeth ever could.

Now you would think that by this time all the little meadow and forest people would have found old Granny Fox out, and that they wouldn't believe her stories. But the truth is most people are very apt to believe unpleasant things about other people without taking the trouble to find out if they are true, and old Granny Fox knows this. Besides, she is smart enough to tell these little trouble-making, untrue stories as if she had heard them from someone else. So, of course, someone else gets the blame for starting them. Oh, Granny Fox is smart and sly! Yes, Siree! She certainly is smart and sly.

It was one of her plans to make trouble that was taking her over to see Prickly Porky the Porcupine. She found him as usual in the top of a poplar tree,

filling his stomach with tender young bark. Granny strolled along as if she had just happened to pass that way and not as if she had come purposely. She pretended to be very much surprised when she looked up and saw Prickly Porky.

"Good morning, Prickly Porky," she said in her pleasantest voice. "How big and fine and strong and brave you are looking this morning!"

Prickly Porky stopped eating and looked down at her suspiciously, but just the same he felt pleased.

"Huh!" he grunted, then once more he began to eat.

Granny Fox went right on talking. "I said when I heard that story this morning that I didn't believe a word of it. I—"

"What story?" Prickly Porky broke in.

"Why, haven't you heard it?" Granny spoke in a tone of great surprise. "Billy Mink told it to me. He said that this

stranger, Old Man Coyote, who has come to the Green Meadows and the Green Forest, has been boasting that he is afraid of nobody, but everybody is afraid of him. When somebody asked him if you were afraid of him, he said that you climbed the highest tree you could find if you but saw his shadow. Of course, I didn't believe it, because I know that you are not afraid of anybody. But other people believe it, and they do say that Old Man Coyote is bragging that the first time he meets you on the ground he is going to have Porcupine for dinner."

Prickly Porky had started down the tree before Granny finished speaking, and his usually dull eyes actually looked bright. The fact is, they were bright with anger. Prickly Porky looked positively fierce.

"What are you going to do?" asked Granny Fox, backing away a little.

"Going to give that boaster a chance to try to get his Porcupine dinner," grunted Prickly Porky.

Granny turned aside to grin. "I don't believe you will find him now," said she, "but I heard that he is planning to get you when you go down to the Laughing Brook for a drink this evening."

"Then I'll wait," grunted Prickly Porky.

So Granny Fox bade him good-by and started on with a wicked chuckle to think how Prickly Porky had believed the story which she had made up.

XII

<hr/>

GRANNY FOX TELLS ANOTHER STORY

Believe all the good that you may hear,
  But always doubt the bad.
Pass on the word of kindly cheer;
  Forget the tale that's sad.

I f everyone would do that what a different world this would be! My, my, my, yes, indeed! There wouldn't be any place for the Granny Foxes who start untrue stories just to make trouble. But we will have to say this much for old Granny Fox—she seldom does make trouble just for the sake of trouble. No, Sir, old Granny Fox seldom, very seldom makes trouble, unless she or Reddy Fox

have something to gain by it. She is too smart and wise for that.

It was just this way now. You see she felt down in her heart that Old Man Coyote the Wolf had no right on the Green Meadows and in the Green Forest. He was a stranger from the Great West, and she felt that she and Reddy Fox had the best right there, because they had been born there and always had lived there; and she was afraid, very much afraid, that there wouldn't be room for them and for Old Man Coyote. But she wasn't big or strong enough to fight him and drive him away, and so the only thing she could think of was to make him so much trouble that he would leave. She had begun by telling an untrue story to Prickly Porky, a story which had made Prickly Porky very angry with Old Man Coyote, although they had never met. Now she was hurrying

down to the Smiling Pool on the banks of which Old Man Coyote was in the habit of taking a sun-bath, she had been told.

Sure enough, when she came in sight of the Smiling Pool, there he lay sprawled out in the sun and talking to Grandfather Frog, who sat on his big green lily-pad well out of reach from the shore. Granny came up on the opposite side of the Smiling Pool from where Old Man Coyote lay.

"How do you do, Mr. Coyote? I have just heard that you have come here to make your home among us, and I am sure we all give you a hearty welcome." Granny said this just as if she really meant it, and all the time she was speaking she was smiling. Old Man Coyote watched her out of half-closed eyes and to himself he thought: "I don't believe a word of it. Granny Fox is too polite, altogether too polite. I wonder what

kind of a trick she is trying to play now." But aloud he said, and his voice was just as smooth and soft and pleasant as Granny's:

"I'm very well, thank you, and I am much obliged to you for your hearty welcome. I am sure we shall be the best of friends."

Now all the time he was saying this, Old Man Coyote was chuckling inside, for he knew well enough that they wouldn't be friends, and that Granny Fox didn't want to be friends. You see, he is quite as sharp as she.

"Yes, indeed, I am sure we shall," replied old Granny Fox. "How big and strong you are, Mr. Coyote! I shouldn't think that you would be afraid of anybody."

Old Man Coyote looked flattered. "I'm not," said he.

Granny Fox raised her eyebrows as if

very much surprised. "Is that so?" she exclaimed. "Why I heard that Prickly Porky the Porcupine is boasting that you are afraid of him and don't dare put your foot in the Green Forest when he is about."

Old Man Coyote suddenly jumped to his feet, and there was an ugly gleam in his yellow eyes. Granny Fox was glad that she was on the other side of the Smiling Pool. "I don't know who this Prickly Porky is," said he, "but if you'll be so kind as to tell me where I can find him, I think I will make him a call at once."

"Probably he's taking a nap in a tree-top just now," replied Granny, "but if you really want to meet him, you'll find him getting a drink at the Laughing Brook in the Green Forest late this afternoon. I do hope that you will be careful, Mr. Coyote."

"Careful! Careful!" snorted he. "There won't be any Prickly Porky when I get through with him!"

"Chug-a-rum!" said Grandfather Frog and looked very hard at old Granny Fox. Granny winked the eye that was nearest to him.

XIII

THE MEETING AT THE LAUGHING BROOK

The trouble with a quarrel is
  That when it's once begun
The whole world tries to push it on,
  And seems to think it fun.

I t usually is anything but fun for those engaged in it, but their neighbors crowd about and urge them on and do their best to make matters worse. It was just that way when Prickly Porcupine and Old Man Coyote met beside the Laughing Brook. Now until they met here neither had ever seen the other, for you know Old Man Coyote had come out of the Great West, while Prickly Porky had come down from the North Woods.

Prickly Porky took one good look and then he grunted, "I'll soon fix him!" What he saw was someone who looked something like a very large gray fox or a dog, and Prickly Porky had put too many foxes and dogs to flight to feel the least bit of fear of the stranger grinning at him and showing all his great teeth.

But Old Man Coyote didn't know what to make of what he saw. Never in all his life had he seen anything like it. He didn't know whether to laugh or to be frightened. About all he could see was what looked like a tremendous great chestnut-burr on legs, which came towards him in little rushes and with a great rattling of the thousand little spears which made him look like a chestnut-burr. Old Man Coyote had never fought with anybody like this, and

66

he didn't know just how to begin. He
didn't like the look of the thousand little
spears. The nearer they came, the less
he liked the look of them. So he backed
away a few steps, growling and snarling
angrily.

Now it seemed that as if by magic the
news that there was trouble between
Prickly Porky and Old Man Coyote had
spread all over the Green Meadows and
through the Green Forest. Everybody
who dared to go was on hand to see it.
Sammy Jay and his cousin, Blacky the
Crow, were there of course, peering
down from the top of a pine-tree and
screaming excitedly. Happy Jack the
Gray Squirrel and Chatterer the Red
Squirrel actually sat side by side in the
same tree, so interested that they forgot
for once to quarrel themselves. Unc'
Billy Possum and Bobby Coon cut their

afternoon nap short and looked on from a safe place in a big chestnut-tree. Danny Meadow Mouse and his cousin, Whitefoot the Wood Mouse, shivered with fright, while they peeped out through a crack in a hollow log. Johnny Chuck came as near as he dared and peeped over the trunk of a fallen tree. Billy Mink and Jerry Muskrat quietly swam up the Laughing Brook and crawled out on the farther bank where they could see and still be safe. Of course Reddy and Granny Fox were there, well hidden so that no one should see them.

And what do you think every one of them was wishing? Why, that Prickly Porky would drive Old Man Coyote away from the Green Forest and off of the Green Meadows. You see, every one of them was afraid of Old Man Coyote, and

right down in his heart each was hoping that Prickly Porky would be able to send Old Man Coyote off yelping, with his face stuck full of little spears as once upon a time he had sent Bowser the Hound.

XIV

SLOW WIT AND QUICK WIT

When Prickly Porky the Porcupine and Old Man Coyote the Prairie Wolf met beside the Laughing Brook, it was a case of Slow Wit meeting Quick Wit. You see, Prickly Porky is very slow in everything he does, that is everything but flipping that queer tail of his about when there is an enemy near enough for it to reach. But in everything else he is oh, so slow! He walks as if he had all the time in the world to get to the place he has started for. He climbs in just the same way. And because he never moves quickly, he never thinks quickly. The fact is, he

doesn't see any need of hurrying, not even in thinking.

But Old Man Coyote is just the opposite. Yes, Sir, he is just the opposite. No one moves quicker than he does. He is nimble on his feet, and his wit is just as quick.

> His nimble wit and nimble feet
> Are very, very hard to beat.

Digger the Badger, who also comes from the Great West, says that to beat Old Man Coyote in anything, you should start the day before he does and not let him know it.

So here was Slow Wit facing Quick Wit, with most of the little meadow people and forest folk looking on. Suddenly Old Man Coyote sprang forward with his ugliest snarl, a snarl that made everybody but Prickly Porky shiver, even

those who were perfectly safe up in the trees.

But Prickly Porky didn't shiver. No, Sir, he just grunted angrily and rattled his thousand little spears.

Now, Old Man Coyote had sprung with that ugly snarl just to try to frighten Prickly Porky, and he had taken care not to spring too close to those rattling spears. When he found that Prickly Porky wasn't frightened the least little bit, he tried another plan. Perhaps he could get Prickly Porky from behind. As quick as a flash and as light as a feather, he leaped right over Prickly Porky and turned to seize him from behind. But he didn't! Oh, my, no! You see, the thousand little spears covered every inch of Prickly Porky's back.

Slowly and clumsily Prickly Porky turned so as to face his enemy.

"Got fooled that time, didn't you, Mr.

Smarty?" he grunted, while his eyes snapped with anger.

Old Man Coyote didn't say anything. He just grinned. But all the time he was using his eyes, and now he discovered that while Prickly Porky was fully protected on his back and sides by the thousand little spears carried in his coat, there wasn't a single little spear in his waistcoat.

"I've got to get him where I can seize him from underneath," thought he, and straightway he began to run in a circle around Prickly Porky while the latter turned slowly round and round, trying to keep his face turned always towards Old Man Coyote. Faster and faster ran Old Man Coyote, and faster and faster turned Prickly Porky. In his slow mind he was trying to understand what it meant, but he couldn't. And for a while the little meadow and forest peo-

73

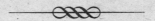

ple looking on were just as much puzzled. It was a most surprising thing. Then suddenly Unc' Billy Possum understood.

"He's trying to make Prickly Porky dizzy," he whispered to Bobby Coon.

"Let's warn Prickly Porky; he'll never think of it himself until it's too late," whispered Bobby Coon.

But before they could do this, the queer performance came to an end. Prickly Porky hadn't discovered what Old Man Coyote was trying to do, but he had become tired of such foolishness, and he suddenly decided to take a rest. So he stopped turning around, and then curled himself up in a ball on the ground, where he looked like a great chestnut-burr. Everybody held their breath to see what Old Man Coyote would do next.

XV

PRICKLY PORKY'S TAIL

Who on a prickly porcupine
  Makes up his mind that he will dine
Must overcome a thousand quills
  Before his stomach Porky fills.
And so it is with you and me;
  With everybody whom we see;
With Reddy Fox and Billy Mink,
  And all the rest of whom we think
On Meadows Green, in Smiling Pool
  Or hidden in the Forest cool:
The thing we've set our hearts upon
  Must past a thousand spears be won.

No one knows this better than did Old Man Coyote as he ran around and around Prickly Porky. He had never felt one of those little spears which Prickly Porky rattled so

fiercely, and he had no mind to feel one. You see, he didn't like the look of them. When finally Prickly Porky lay down and curled up into a great prickly ball, like a huge chestnut-burr, Old Man Coyote sat down just a little way off to study how he was going to get at Prickly Porky without getting hurt by some of those sharp, barbed little spears.

For a long time he sat and studied and studied, his tongue hanging out of one side of his mouth. Once he looked up at Sammy Jay and Blacky the Crow and winked, but he didn't make a sound. Sammy and Blacky chuckled to themselves and winked back, and for a wonder they didn't make a sound. Somehow that wink made them have more of a friendly feeling for Old Man Coyote. You see, that wink told them that Old Man Coyote was just the same kind of a sly

rogue as themselves, and so right away they had a fellow feeling for him.

And none of the little meadow and forest people looking on made a sound. Some of them didn't dare to, and others were so anxious to see what would happen next that they didn't want to. It was so still that the little leaves up in the tree-tops could be heard whispering good night to the Merry Little Breezes, for whom Old Mother West Wind was waiting with her big bag out on the Green Meadows to take them to their home behind the Purple Hills. It was so still that after a while Prickly Porky began to wonder if he were all alone. You see, being curled up that way, he couldn't see and had to trust to his ears. He waited a little longer, and then he uncurled just enough to peep out. There sat Old Man Coyote, and Prickly Porky promptly curled up again.

Now the minute he curled up again something happened. Old Man Coyote looked up at Sammy Jay and Blacky the Crow and winked once more. Then very softly, so softly that he didn't so much as rustle a leaf, he tiptoed around to the other side of Prickly Porky and sat down just as before.

"Now," thought he, "when he peeps out again, he will think I have gone, and then perhaps I can catch him by surprise."

Bobby Coon saw through his plan right away. "Someone ought to warn Prickly Porky," he whispered to Unc' Billy Possum.

Unc' Billy shook his head. "No," he whispered back, "No, Brer Coon! That wouldn't be fair. It's they-all's quarrel and not ours, and though Ah done want to see Brer Porky win just as much as yo' do, Ah reckon it wouldn't be right fo'

78

us to meddle. They-all done got to fight it out themselves."

For a long time nothing happened. Then Old Man Coyote grew tired of waiting. Very carefully he crept nearer and nearer, with his nose stretched out to sniff at that prickly ball on the ground. Everybody held his breath, for everybody remembered what had happened to Bowser the Hound when he came sniffing around Prickly Porky—how Prickly Porky's tail had suddenly slapped Bowser full in the face, filling it with sharp little spears. Now they hoped to see the same thing happen to Old Man Coyote. So they held their breath as they kept their eyes on Old Man Coyote and Prickly Porky's tail.

XVI

OLD MAN COYOTE'S SMARTNESS

When you meet an adversary
  Bold and brave be, also wary.

If the weapons you may hear of,
  Teeth and claws, you have no fear of,

Don't be heedless and rush blindly
  Lest you be received unkindly,

And, like Prickly Porky, find him
  With a dangerous tail behind him.

Now Old Man Coyote knew nothing about that dangerous tail. He had never heard how Bowser the Hound had been sent yelping home with his face stuck full of those sharp lit-

tle spears. But Old Man Coyote is wary. Oh, my, yes! He certainly is wary. To be wary, you know, is to be very, very careful where you go and what you do until you know for sure that there is no possible danger. And there is no one more wary than Old Man Coyote, not even wise, sly, old Granny Fox.

So now, though Prickly Porky, curled up in a ball in front of him, looked harmless enough except for the thousand little spears sticking out all over him, Old Man Coyote was too wary—too smart and too careful—to take any chances as Bowser the Hound had rashly done. And this is why, as he stole forward with his nose stretched out as if to sniff of Prickly Porky, he suddenly stopped just when the little meadow and forest people looking on were holding their breath and hugging themselves with joy and excitement because they expected to see the

81

same thing happen to Old Man Coyote that had happened to Bowser.

Yes, Sir, Old Man Coyote stopped. He studied Prickly Porky a few minutes. Then slowly he walked around him, just studying and studying.

"It looks safe enough to go closer and sniff at him," thought Old Man Coyote, "but I learned a long time ago that you cannot always tell just by looks, and that the most harmless looking thing is some-times the most dangerous. Now it looks to me as if this stupid Porcupine couldn't hurt a flea so long as he keeps curled up this way, but I don't *know*, and I'm not going any nearer until I do know."

He scratched his head thoughtfully, and then he had an idea. He began to dig in the soft earth.

"What under the sun is he doing that for?" whispered Happy Jack Squirrel to his cousin, Chatterer the Red Squirrel.

"I don't know," replied Chatterer, also in a whisper. "We'll probably know in a few minutes."

He had hardly finished when Old Man Coyote threw a little lump of earth so that it hit Prickly Porky. Now, of course Prickly Porky couldn't see what was going on, because, you know, he was curled up with his head tucked down in his waistcoat. But he had been listening as hard as ever he could, and he had heard Old Man Coyote's footsteps very close to him. When the little lump of earth struck him, he thought it was Old Man Coyote himself, and like a flash he slapped that queer tail of his around. Of course it didn't hit anybody, because there was nobody within reach. But it told Old Man Coyote all that he wanted to know.

"Ha, ha, ha!" he laughed. "That's the time I fooled you instead of you fooling

me! You've got to get up early to fool me with a trick like that, Mr. Smarty!"

Then what do you think he did? Why, he just scooped earth on to Prickly Porky as fast as he could dig. Prickly Porky stood it for a few minutes, but he didn't want to be buried alive. Besides, now that his trick was found out by the smartness of Old Man Coyote, there was no use in keeping still any longer. So, with a grunt of anger, Prickly Porky scrambled to his feet, and rattling his thousand little spears, rushed at Old Man Coyote, who just jumped to one side, laughing fit to kill himself.

XVII

―∞∞∞―

GRANNY FOX IS FOUND OUT

Granny Fox is sly and wise
  And seldom taken by surprise,
But wisdom wrongly put to use
  Can never find a good excuse.
It ceases then to wisdom be,
  But foolishness, as we shall see.

Now, with all her smartness and all her cleverness, Old Granny Fox had made one great mistake. Yes, Sir, old Granny Fox had made one great mistake. You see, she had become so used to being thought the smartest and cleverest of all the little people who lived on the Green Meadows and around the Smiling Pool and in the Green Forest, that she had come to be-

lieve that there couldn't be anybody anywhere as smart and clever as she. That was because she didn't know Old Man Coyote. And now, as she and Reddy Fox watched from their hiding place the meeting between Old Man Coyote and Prickly Porky, she felt a sudden sharp sting in her pride. Old Man Coyote had proved himself too smart for Prickly Porky. She ground her teeth as she heard him laughing fit to kill himself as he kept out of Prickly Porky's reach, and she ground them still more as she heard him say:

"You will boast that you will drive me out of the Green Forest, will you, Mr. Porcupine? The time to brag will be when you have done it."

Prickly Porky stopped short in the middle of one of his clumsy rushes.

"Boaster and bragger yourself!" he grunted. "You don't seem to be dining on

Porcupine the first time we meet. Why don't you? Why don't you make your own boast good?"

Old Man Coyote stopped laughing and pricked up his ears. "What's that?" he demanded. "What's that? Somebody has been filling your ears with something that is very like a lie, Mr. Porcupine."

"No more than they have yours, Mr. Coyote," replied Prickly Porky, letting his thousand little spears drop part way back into his coat. "But Old Granny Fox told me."

"Ha! So it was Granny Fox!" interrupted Old Man Coyote. "So it was old Granny Fox! Well, it was that same old mischief-maker who told me that—" He stopped and suddenly looked very hard at the very place where Granny and Reddy were hiding. Then he made a long jump in that direction. Granny and Reddy didn't wait for him. They started

for home so fast that they looked like nothing but two little red streaks disappearing among the trees.

"Ha, ha, ha! Ho, ho, ho! Hee, hee, hee! Ha, ho, he, ho!" laughed Old Man Coyote, and all the little meadow and forest people who were looking on laughed with him. Then he turned to Prickly Porky.

"I guess you and I are going to be friends," said he.

"I guess we are," replied Prickly Porky, and all his little spears dropped out of sight.

XVIII

THE CUNNING OF OLD GRANNY FOX

You must get up very early,
  You must lie awake at night,
You must have your wits well sharpened
  And your eyes must be so bright
That there's nothing can escape them,
  Nothing that you do not see,
If ahead of Granny Fox you
  Ever get, or hope to be.

Happy Jack Squirrel made up that verse one day after he had had oh, such a narrow escape from old Granny Fox. It had made Happy Jack very sober for a while, for Granny had so nearly caught him that she actually had pulled some hair from Happy Jack's tail. All the other little for-

est and meadow people agreed that Happy Jack was quite right. Most of them had had just such narrow escapes from Old Granny Fox.

You see, it is this way: Old Granny Fox is very, very cunning. To be cunning, you know, is to be sly and smart in doing things in such a way as no one else will think of doing them. Just now, the thing that Granny wanted most of anything in the world was to drive Old Man Coyote away from the Green Meadows and the Green Forest. She couldn't do it openly, because he was bigger and stronger than she, so she had thought and thought and thought, trying to find some plan which might get Old Man Coyote into trouble, so that he would go away and stay away.

Then Reddy Fox told her that he had found the place where Old Man Coyote took a sun-nap every day and a splendid plan came to Granny. At least, it seemed

like a splendid plan. The more she thought about it, the better it seemed.

But Granny Fox never acts hastily. She is too wise for that. So she studied and studied this plan that she had thought of to make trouble for Old Man Coyote. Finally she was satisfied.

"I believe it will work. I certainly do believe it will work," said she, and called Reddy Fox over to her.

"I want you to make sure that Old Man Coyote takes his sun-nap in the same place every day," said she. "You must see him there yourself. It won't do to take the word of anyone else for it. I want you to steal up every day and make sure that he is there. Be sure you don't tell anyone, not anyone at all, what you are doing, and above all things, don't let *him* get so much as a glimpse of you."

Reddy promised that he would take the greatest care, and so for a week ev-

ery day he crept to a snug hiding-place behind a thick clump of grass where he could peep through and see Old Man Coyote taking his sun-nap. Then he would tiptoe softly away and hurry to report to old Granny Fox.

"Good!" she would say. "Go again to-morrow and make sure that he is there."

"But what do you want to know for?" Reddy asked one day, for he was becoming very, very curious.

"Never mind what I want to know for," replied Granny severely. "Do as I tell you, and you will find out soon enough."

You see, Granny Fox was too cunning to let even Reddy know of her plan, for if no one but herself knew it, it couldn't possibly leak out, and that, you know, is the only way to keep a secret.

XIX

———⊰⊱⊰⊱———

Bowser the Hound Has a Visitor

Bowser the Hound lay in Farmer Brown's dooryard dozing in the sun. Bowser was dreaming. Yes, Sir, Bowser was dreaming. Farmer Brown's boy, passing through the yard on his way to the cornfield, laughed.

"Sic him, Bowser! Sic him! That's the dog! Don't let him fool you this time," said he.

You see, Bowser was talking in his sleep. He was whining eagerly, and every once in a while breaking out into excited little yelps, and so Farmer Brown's boy knew that he was dreaming that he was hunting, that he was on the trail of Reddy Fox or sly old Granny Fox. His

eyes were shut, and he didn't hear what
Farmer Brown's boy said. The latter
went off laughing, his hoe on his shoulder, for there was work for him down in
the cornfield.

Bowser kept right on getting more and
more excited. It was a splendid hunt he
was having there in dreamland. Across
the Green Meadows, along the edge
of the Green Forest, and up through the
Old Pasture he ran, all in his dream, you
know, and just ahead of him ran old
Granny Fox. Not once was he fooled by
her tricks, and she tried every one she
knew. For once he was too smart for her,
and it made him tingle all over with delight, for he was sure that this time he
would catch her.

And then something queer happened.
Yes, Sir, it was something very queer indeed. He saw Granny Fox stop just a little way ahead of him. She sat down

facing him and began to laugh at him. She laughed and laughed fit to kill herself. It made Bowser very angry. Oh, very angry indeed. No one likes to be laughed at, you know, and to be laughed at by Granny Fox of all people was more than Bowser could stand. He opened his mouth to give a great roar as he sprang at her and then—why, Bowser waked up. Yes, Sir, he really had given a great roar, and had waked himself up with his own voice.

For a few minutes Bowser winked and blinked, for the sun was shining in his eyes. Then he winked and blinked some more, but not because of the sun. Oh, my, no! It wasn't because of the sun that he winked and blinked now. It was because—what do you think? Why, it was because Bowser the Hound couldn't tell whether he was awake or asleep. He thought that he was awake. He was sure

that he was awake, and yet—well, there sat old Granny Fox laughing at him, just as she had seen her in his dream. Yes, Sir, there she sat, laughing at him. Poor Bowser! He just didn't know what to think. He rubbed both eyes and looked. There she sat, laughing just as before. Bowser closed his eyes tight and kept them closed for a whole minute. Perhaps when he opened them again, she would be gone. Then he would know that she was only a dream fox, after all.

But no, Sir! When he opened his eyes again, there she sat, laughing harder than ever. Just then a hen came around a corner of the house. Granny Fox stopped laughing. Like a flash she caught the hen, slung her over her shoulder and trotted away, all the time keeping one eye on Bowser.

Then Bowser knew that this was no dream fox, but old Granny Fox herself,

and that she had had the impudence and boldness to steal a hen right under his very nose! He was awake now, was Bowser, very much awake. With a great roar of anger, he sprang to his feet, and started after Granny, and startled the Merry Little Breezes at play on the Green Meadows.

XX

THE CLEVER PLAN OF GRANNY FOX

The bold visit of old Granny Fox to Bowser the Hound in Farmer Brown's dooryard right in broad daylight was all a part of the clever plan Granny had worked out to make trouble for Old Man Coyote. First she had sent Reddy Fox to make sure that Old Man Coyote was taking his usual sun-nap in his usual place. If he were, Reddy was to softly steal away and then hurry to the top of the Crooked Little Path where it comes down the hill. When he got there, he was to bark three times. Granny was to be hidden behind the old stone wall on the edge of Farmer Brown's orchard, and when she heard Reddy bark, she was to

do her part, while Reddy was to hide in a secret place on the edge of the Green Forest and watch what would happen.

It all turned out just as Granny had planned. She had been in hiding behind the old stone wall only a few minutes when she heard Reddy bark three times. Granny grinned. Then she stole up to Farmer Brown's dooryard, and there she found Bowser the Hound fast asleep and dreaming. She was just getting ready to bark to waken him, when he waked himself with his own voice. It was just then that a hen happened to walk around the corner of the house. Granny's eyes sparkled. "Good," said she to herself. "I'll take this hen along with me, and Reddy and I will have a good dinner after I have set Bowser to chasing Old Man Coyote"—for that was what Granny was planning to do. So she caught the hen, threw it over her shoulder, and started

off with Bowser the Hound after her, making a great noise with his big voice.

Now, of course Granny knew that she couldn't carry that hen very far and keep ahead of Bowser, so she ran straight across the Old Orchard towards the secret place on the edge of the Green Forest where she knew that Reddy Fox was hiding. When she was sure that Reddy could see her, she gave the hen a toss over into the grass and then raced away towards the Green Meadows. You see, she knew that Bowser would keep on right after her, and when it was safe for him to do so, Reddy would steal out from his hiding place and get the hen, and that is just what did happen.

Away ran Granny, and after her ran Bowser, and all the little meadow and forest people heard his great voice and were glad that he was not after them. But Granny Fox was not worried. You

see, she had fooled him so many times that she knew she could do it again. So she kept just a little way ahead of him and gradually led him towards the place where Old Man Coyote took his sun-nap every day. But she was too smart to run straight towards it, "For," said she to herself, "if I do that, he will become alarmed and run away before Bowser is near enough to see him." So she ran in a big circle around the place, feeling sure that Old Man Coyote would lie perfectly still so as not to be seen.

Round and round ran Granny Fox with Bowser after her, and all the time she was making the circles smaller and smaller so as to get nearer and nearer to the napping-place of Old Man Coyote. When she thought that she was near enough, she suddenly started straight for it.

"Now," thought she, "he'll jump and

run, and when Bowser sees him, he will forget all about me. He will follow Old Man Coyote, and perhaps he will drive him away from the Green Meadows forever."

Nearer and nearer to the napping place Granny drew. She was almost there. Why didn't Old Man Coyote jump and run? At last she was right to it. She could see just where he had been stretched out, but he wasn't there now. There wasn't a sign of him anywhere! What did it mean? Just then she heard a sound over in the Green Forest that made her grind her teeth with rage.

"Ha, ha, ha! Ho, ho, ho! Hee, hee, hee! Ha, ho, hee, ho!" It was the laughter of Old Man Coyote.

XXI

How Peter Rabbit Helped Old Man Coyote

A kindly word, a kindly deed,
  Is like the planting of a seed;
It first sends forth a little root
  And by and by bears splendid fruit.

When Old Man Coyote first came to the Green Meadows, to live, he chased Peter Rabbit and gave Peter a terrible fright. After that for some time Peter kept very close to the dear Old Briar-patch, where he always felt perfectly safe. But Peter dearly loves to roam, and Peter is very, very curious, so it wasn't long before he began to grow tired of the Old Briar-patch and long to go abroad on the Green Meadows

and in the Green Forest as he always had done, and find out all that was going on among his neighbors.

Of course Peter heard a great deal, for Sammy Jay and Blacky the Crow would stop almost every day to tell him the latest news about Old Man Coyote. They told him all about how Granny Fox had tried to make trouble between him and Prickly Porky the Porcupine, and how she had been found out. After they had gone, Peter sat very still for a long time, thinking it all over.

"H-m-m," said Peter to himself, "it is very plain to me that Old Man Coyote is smarter than Granny Fox, and that means a great deal to me. Yes, Sir, that means a great deal to me. It means that I have got to watch out for him even sharper than I have to watch out for Granny and Reddy Fox. Dear me, dear

me, just as if I didn't have troubles enough as it is!"

As he talked, Peter was sitting on the very edge of the Old Briar-patch, looking towards the place where Sammy Jay had told him that Old Man Coyote took his sun-nap every day. Suddenly he saw something that made him stop thinking about his troubles and sit up a little straighter and open his big eyes a little wider. It was Reddy Fox, creeping very, very slowly and carefully towards the napping place of Old Man Coyote. When he was near enough to see, Reddy lay down in the grass and watched. After a little while he tiptoed back to the Green Forest.

Peter scratched his long left ear with his long right hind foot. "Now what did Reddy Fox do that for?" he said, thoughtfully.

The next day and the next day and the

105

day after that, Peter saw Reddy Fox do the same thing, and all the time Peter's curiosity grew and grew and grew. He didn't say anything about it to anyone, but just puzzled and puzzled over it.

Late that afternoon Peter heard footsteps just outside the Old Briar-patch. Peeping out, he saw Old Man Coyote passing. Peter's curiosity could be kept down no longer.

"How do you do, Mr. Coyote?" said Peter in a very small and frightened sounding voice, but in a very polite manner.

Old Man Coyote stopped and peeped through the brambles. "Hello, Peter Rabbit," said he. "I haven't had the pleasure of meeting you outside of the Old Briar-patch for some time." He grinned when he said this in a way that showed all his long sharp teeth.

"No," replied Peter, "I—I—well, you

see, I'm afraid of Old Granny and Reddy Fox."

Old Man Coyote grinned again, for he knew that it was himself Peter really feared. "Pooh, Peter Rabbit! You shouldn't be afraid of them!" said he. "They're not very smart. You ought to be able to keep out of their way."

Peter hopped a little nearer to the edge of the Old Briar-patch. "Tell me, Mr. Coyote, what is Reddy Fox watching you for every day when you take your sun-nap?"

"What's that?" demanded Old Man Coyote sharply.

He listened gravely while Peter told him what he had seen. When Peter had finished, Mr. Coyote smiled, and somehow this time he didn't show all those dreadful teeth.

"Thank you, Peter Rabbit," said he.

107

"You have done me a great favor, and I hope I can return it some time. Do you know, I believe that we are going to be friends."

And with that Old Man Coyote went on his way, chuckling to himself.

XXII

WHY THE CLEVER PLAN OF GRANNY FOX FAILED

When Old Man Coyote, chuckling to himself, left Peter Rabbit and the Old Briar-patch, he went straight over to look around the place where he took his sun-nap every day. His sharp eyes soon saw the place where Reddy Fox had been lying in the grass to watch him, for of course the grass was pressed down by the weight of Reddy's body.

"Peter Rabbit told me the truth, sure enough, and I guess I owe him a good turn," muttered Old Man Coyote, as he studied and studied to see why Reddy was watching him every day. You see, he is so sharp and clever himself that he

was sure right away that Reddy had some plan in mind to bring him to the same place every day.

But he didn't let on that he knew anything about what was going on. Oh, my, no! The next day he curled up for his sun-nap just as usual, only this time he took care to lie in such a way that he would be looking towards Reddy's hiding place. Then he pretended to go to sleep, but if you had been there and looked into his eyes, you would have found no sleepy-winks there. No, Sir, you wouldn't have found one single sleepy-wink! Instead, his eyes were as bright as if there were no such thing as sleep. He saw Reddy steal out of the Green Forest. Then he closed his eyes all but just a tiny little crack, through which he could see Reddy's hiding place, but all the time he looked as if his eyes were shut tight.

Reddy crept softly as he could, which

is very softly indeed, to his hiding place and lay down to watch. Old Man Coyote pretended to be very fast asleep, and every once in a while he would make believe snore. But all the time he was watching Reddy. After a little while Reddy tiptoed away until he felt sure that it was safe to run. Then he hurried as fast as he could go to report to Old Granny Fox in the Green Forest. Old Man Coyote chuckled as he watched Reddy disappear.

"I don't know what it all means," said he, "but if he and old Granny Fox think that they are going to catch me napping, they are making one of the biggest mistakes of their lives."

The next day and the next the same thing happened, but the day after that Reddy only stopped long enough to make sure that Old Man Coyote was there just as usual, and then he hurried away to

the top of the Crooked Little Path that comes down the hill. There he barked three times. Old Man Coyote watched him go and heard him bark.

"That's some kind of a signal," said he to himself, "and unless I am greatly mistaken, it means mischief. I think I won't take a nap to-day, for I want to see what is going on."

With that, Old Man Coyote made a very long leap off to one side, then two more, so as to leave no scent to show which way he had gone. Then, chuckling to himself, he hurried to the Green Forest and hid where he could watch Reddy Fox. He saw Reddy hide on the edge of the Green Forest where he could watch Farmer Brown's dooryard, and then he crept up where he could watch too. Of course he saw old Granny Fox when she led Bowser the Hound down across the Green Meadows, and he guessed right

away what her plan was. It tickled him
so that he had to clap both hands over
his mouth as he watched sly old Granny take Bowser straight over to his
napping-place, and when he saw how
surprised she was to find him gone he
sat up and laughed until all the little
people on the Green Meadows and in the
Green Forest heard him and wondered
what could be tickling Old Man Coyote
so.

XXIII

OLD MAN COYOTE GETS A GOOD DINNER

When old Granny Fox found that Old Man Coyote was not at his usual napping-place, she was sure that Reddy Fox must have been very stupid and thought that he saw him there when he didn't. She hurried to the Laughing Brook and waded in it for a little way in order to destroy her scent so that Bowser the Hound would not know in which direction she had gone. You know water is always the friend of little animals who leave scent in their footsteps. Bowser came baying up to the edge of the Laughing Brook, and there he stopped, for his wonderful nose could not follow Granny in the water and he

could not tell whether she had gone up or down or across the brook.

But Bowser is not one to give up easily. No, indeed! He had learned many of Granny's tricks, and now he knew well enough what Granny had done. At least, Bowser thought that he knew.

"She'll wade a little way, and then she will come out of the water, so all I have to do is to find the place where she has come out, and there I will find her tracks again," said he, and with his nose to the ground he hurried down one bank of the Laughing Brook.

He went as far as he thought Granny could have waded, but there was no trace of her. Then he crossed the brook, and with his nose still to the ground, ran back to the starting place along the other bank.

"She didn't go down the brook, so she must have gone up," said Bowser, and

started up the brook as eagerly as he had gone down. After running as far as he thought Granny could possibly have waded, Bowser crossed over and ran back along the other bank to the starting place without finding any trace of Granny Fox. At last, with a foolish and ashamed air, Bowser gave it up and started for home, and all the time Granny Fox was lying in plain sight, watching him. Yes, Sir, she was watching him and laughing to herself. You see, she knew perfectly well that Bowser depends more on his nose than on his eyes, and that when he is running with his nose to the ground, he can see very little about him. So she had simply waded down the Laughing Brook to a flat rock in the middle of it, and on this she had stretched herself out and kept perfectly still. Twice Bowser had gone right past without seeing her. She enjoyed seeing

him fooled so much that for the time being she quite forgot about Old Man Coyote and the failure of her clever plan to make trouble for him.

But when Bowser the Hound had gone, Granny remembered. She stopped laughing, and a look of angry disappointment crossed her face as she trotted towards home. But as she trotted along, her face cleared a little. "Anyway, Reddy and I will have a good dinner on that fat hen I caught in Farmer Brown's dooryard," she muttered.

When she reached home, there sat Reddy on the doorstep, but there was no sign of the fat hen, and Reddy looked very uneasy and frightened.

"Where's that fat hen I caught?" demanded Granny crossly.

"I—I—I'm sorry, Granny, but I haven't got it," said Reddy.

"Haven't got it!" snapped Granny.

"What's the matter with you, Reddy Fox? Didn't you see me throw it in the grass when I ran past the place where you were hiding, and didn't you know enough to go and get it?"

"Yes," replied Reddy, "I saw you throw it in the grass, and I went out and got it, but on my way home I met someone who took it away from me."

"Took it away from you!" exclaimed Granny. "Who was it? Tell me this instant! Who was it?"

"Old Man Coyote," replied Reddy in a low, frightened voice.

Old Granny Fox simply stared at Reddy. She couldn't find a word to say. Instead of making trouble for Old Man Coyote, she had furnished him with a good dinner. He was smarter than she. She decided then and there that she could not drive Old Man Coyote out of the Green Forest and that she would ei-

ther have to leave herself or accept him and make the best of it.

But that's what Old Man Coyote had thought all along, for he quite liked his new home and took a good deal of interest in his new neighbors.

One of these whom he found most interesting was Paddy the Beaver. Paddy really is a very wonderful fellow and I will tell you about him in the next book.